"You have to be kidding," Linda Jean whispered angrily to me. "You're late, and then you forget all your stuff for the party, too? Why did you even bother to come?"

Linda Jean turned to Krissy. "What are we going to do with the last half hour of the party?" she asked.

"What about...?" I started to ask as I walked up behind them.

They kept their backs to me.

"Forget it." Krissy said. "You've done enough damage already. We'll figure out something. Why don't you go back to Graham and the TV studio?"

"Because I'm a part of this business, and I'm here to help," I replied sternly.

"You could have fooled me," Krissy answered angrily.

"You're going to have to choose," Linda Jean said. "It's either the Forever Friends Club or Graham and the studio. You don't have time for both!"

# Keeping Secrets,
# Keeping Friends!

Cindy Savage

Cover illustration by Richard Kriegler

*To Laura—*
*with Love*

Published by Willowisp Press, Inc.
401 E. Wilson Bridge Road, Worthington, Ohio 43085

Printed in the United States of America
10 9 8 7 6 5 4 3 2 1

ISBN 0-87406-413-9

# One

"I'M sorry I'm late," I said as I breezed into Joy's living room. "I got hung up at the TV studio. What have I missed?"

The regular afternoon meeting of the Forever Friends Club was already in progress. Joy Marshall, Krissy Branch, Linda Jean Jacobs, and I, Aimee Lawrence, are the club's members. We usually get along great, but that day I could tell that something was wrong. They were upset with me.

"You've been late a lot lately," Linda Jean said. "You know when our meetings start. So, what's the problem, Aimee?"

Then Krissy spoke up. "Yeah. You've been late three times this week, and another zillion times last month. The rest of us show up on time, and then we have to sit around

5

waiting for you so we can talk about business."

The business they were talking about is Party Time. Ever since last June when Linda Jean came up with the idea, the Forever Friends Club has been giving parties for younger kids. It has been really fun. And we made lots of money over the summer, too.

But this wasn't the happy group that had marched arm in arm to the bank last week. Krissy was frowning at me. Linda Jean was looking angrily out the window. And Joy kept busy sewing up one of her dance costumes so she wouldn't have to look in my direction.

The three of them took up all the space on the couch, so I sat down in the straight-backed chair across the room. I felt like I was on trial, and I was facing the jury.

"I said I was sorry," I repeated, staring at each of them. "I couldn't help it. Graham needed me to help him get the props together for tomorrow's show. I couldn't leave him right in the middle of everything."

"Well, we need you at these meetings to help make decisions about parties and schedules and supplies and stuff. The rest of us sit around and waste our time while you're off with Graham," Linda Jean complained.

"Doesn't that matter to you?"

"Of course, it does," I said.

"And ever since you met Graham when we did that TV special, you spend all your time at the studio," Krissy added.

"You're the ones who wanted me to be friends with him in the first place," I countered. "If you'll remember, I told him I didn't have time to do anything with him. But, no, you told me that I should give him a chance. So, I changed my mind."

"That's not the point," Joy said. "We're glad you're friends with Graham. And we're glad you have so much fun working at the studio. But Party Time is an equal partnership. If one of us doesn't do her job, the whole thing falls apart."

I crossed my arms. "Are you accusing me of not doing my job?" I asked defensively.

"Not really. You just have been neglecting it a little," said Krissy.

"Look," Joy interrupted. "Let's remember what the Forever Friends Club is all about. We've known each other a long time. We've always been able to work around each other's schedules. You all cover for me when I have to go to a dance recital. Sometimes Linda Jean has to take her animals to the veterinarian or give them extra care, or Krissy has to go along with her sister during modeling trips. We always find a way to manage everything."

"You're right," Linda Jean said. "And we'll work this out, too."

"I guess schedules are getting pretty rough for all of us since school started last week. I don't know about you guys, but I have homework up to my ears already," Joy remarked. "We're going to have to cut down on the number of parties we give if we're going to do well in our classes this year."

"I admit that working as a volunteer at the TV station has made my schedule even tighter," I put in. "But it's something that I really like doing."

"We already know that you have stars in your eyes," Linda Jean teased, sounding more like her normal self. When I looked over at her, she was smiling.

"Why don't we hold the club meetings an hour later in the afternoon?" suggested Krissy. "That way, Aimee won't be late. And we won't have to sit around waiting for her."

Joy held up her hand for silence. "Okay, we'll meet here right after school as usual. But instead of having the club meeting right away, we'll do homework or help Abby or whatever. Or, if there's something else any of us has to do, that's okay, too. How does that sound?"

We all nodded our heads. Krissy smiled at me. I felt better. I really hate arguing—especially when I know the other person is probably right.

I admit that I had been spending a lot of time at WBCC, where my dad hosts *Weekend Mag*, a local happenings show. Party Time was featured on his show last July. At first, we all had been nervous to go on TV. But the show turned out great, and business really boomed after our appearance. Of course, it's great that Graham Moore worked there, too.

Graham is the neatest boy I've ever met. He's serious and funny at the same time. His mom, Jackie Moore, is the producer for my dad's show. When Graham moved in with her after having lived with his father for most of his life, she gave him a job at the studio. He works as a "gofer," which means that he "goes for" anything people on the staff need in order to do their jobs. Graham's mom pays him an allowance for doing his job because he's only in the eighth grade, which means he's too young to work for real.

And besides getting to know Graham, I loved being around the lights, the camera, and all the activity. I loved the smell of the stage and the way all the stagehands ran around announcing commercials and setting up camera angles. I couldn't think of anything more exciting than working at a television studio.

But my big dream is to sing professionally someday. That is my ultimate goal. But I also love designing clothes and sewing what I have created. Being original is my specialty.

I also think teaching children could be fun. When I sing songs or work on craft projects with a bunch of kids, it seems like the best job in the whole world. I guess I like a lot of things right now. I'm glad I'm only in the seventh grade and don't have to decide on a career yet.

Krissy's voice interrupted my thoughts. "We've been talking about slowing down, but I don't think it's going to happen for a while. Just look at this list of parties we've scheduled."

She held up the large square calendar where we write down the parties we book.

"The TV show really gave us a lot of business. We are still getting calls about it," Joy added.

"Look," Krissy said. "We have four parties booked this weekend and three next weekend. The rest of the month is about the same."

"So, we haven't slowed down. We've just squeezed what was a week's worth of parties in the summer into the two weekend days during the school year. When am I going to do my homework?" Joy moaned. "School has only been going on for a week, but I'm already buried under a mountain of social studies and science homework. Every teacher expects an hour of work from us each night. Even without using a calculator, I know there aren't enough hours in the day to do everything I'm supposed to do."

That was the understatement of the year. I felt even more frustrated than Joy did.

We spent the next two hours helping Abby make hors d'oeuvres for the next party she was catering. The Forever Friends Club also works for Joy's mom, Abby. Her catering service actually helped Party Time get started. Now we entertain at some of her events, and she caters some of our parties. The arrangement works out perfectly.

As we rolled dough and stuffed mushrooms, we talked about what we would need for the parties we were giving on Saturday. The first party had a pirate theme, and the second had a Cinderella theme.

I was exhausted by the time I saw my mom's car drive into Joy's driveway to pick me up. It was the first time in a long time that I was glad to go home from a Forever Friends Club meeting.

After school the next day, Graham and I rode our bikes to the studio together. It was neat that Graham had transferred to our school. When his mom decided to move, they thought Graham would be going to Piedmont Junior High. But his mother picked out a house closer to the studio, which meant he would go to Martin Luther King with us.

Graham was quiet as we wound our way past overhanging magnolia trees. Like so many Atlanta streets, these didn't have sidewalks, but there was plenty of room to ride our bikes safely through the neighborhoods.

"Is something bothering you, Graham?" I asked.

"No. Why do you ask?" Graham replied curiously.

"You just don't seem like your usual self today. Aren't you looking forward to the weekend?" I asked.

"Sure, I guess I am," he said slowly. "It's just that starting school reminds me of my father. I've gone to a lot of different schools. It will be strange to stay in one place for all of junior high and high school."

"I've lived in Atlanta all my life," I said. "You're lucky to have lived in so many different places. I've just gone places on vacation. But you've actually lived other places. That's exciting."

"Atlanta is different from any of the countries or towns I've lived in before, though. It's bigger. You have to transfer buses three times to get downtown. And the school is a lot bigger, too. I hope I can find a few friends, learn to survive in the cafeteria—stuff like that."

"Well, you can count on Joy, Krissy, Linda Jean, and me to be your friends," I told him reassuringly. At least, I hoped my Forever Friends would want to be Graham's friend, too.

"Thanks. I appreciate it," he said with a little smile.

We rolled up to the bike racks outside of

the WBCC TV studio. I uncoiled my lock from under my seat and watched Graham closely as he did the same.

Graham is taller than most boys our age. He told me jokingly once that he grew so fast because he had to eat so many types of foreign food as he moved from country to country with his father. Mr. Moore is a photojournalist for *National Geographic* magazine.

Graham has a sunny smile. It can really light up a room. And he definitely needed his cheerful personality that afternoon, because we could hear shouting all the way from the lobby. It looked like we were in for a hectic time.

"Hey, Dave! Bring that camera over to the left," we heard Frank shout. Frank was *Weekend Mag's* director.

"Have someone move the light cords, and then I'll move the camera!" Dave, the camera operator, yelled back. "Where's maintenance?"

"How should I know? I'm trying to get a show taped, not scrub the floor!" yelled Frank.

"Hey, we air this segment tomorrow evening," Dave continued. "Where's Aimee? Where's Graham? We need the script and cue cards set up."

"Coming right up, sir," Graham said, flashing a smile in Dave's direction.

"Why are they using cue cards?" I asked. "What happened to the TV screen that they read the scripts from?"

"It's in the shop for a few weeks. Until it's fixed, we have to do it the old-fashioned way, with cards."

Dave gave us a look that told us to be quiet. I set my backpack down on a shelf and followed Graham. "What can I do?" I whispered. Everyone was setting up for the first take, and I didn't want to get into any more trouble for making noise.

Graham looked at the script he held in one hand and the cue cards he had scooped up in the other hand. "I'll deliver the props. You organize the cue cards with the script," he suggested.

I quickly began checking the script and arranging the large boards with large print on them in the same order as the planned dialogue. Out of the corner of my eye, I could see Graham running toward the prop room.

I set the cue cards on their stand and stepped backward out of the way to watch all the action. Dad waved at me as he took his seat in the large blue chair that was one of his trademarks.

"Did you have a good day at school?" he asked me as the countdown clock ticked off the seconds that would signal the beginning of filming.

I smiled and nodded. "I got an A on my history pop quiz."

"That's my girl," he said with a big smile.

"Okay. We're ready to roll!" yelled one of the camera operators.

Dad straightened up, adjusted his tie, and put on his talk show host smile. It was a nice, friendly smile. That's why Gerald Lawrence was one of the most popular personalities on local television. People felt that they could trust him.

Graham has the same contagious smile as my dad has. I think I can trust him, too.

# *Two*

THE weekend was a blur of activity, with back-to-back parties on Saturday and Sunday. Because of all the crafts I was doing at the parties, I felt like I was living with a pair of scissors in my hand.

"Well, I'm glad that's over," I said, as we finished our final cleanup after our fourth party of the weekend.

"I don't think we've ever had a more fun party, though," Joy remarked. "I loved the expression on Leann's face when the treasure box opened and all the helium balloons flew out. It was wonderful."

Even though I am usually tired after the parties end, I always enjoy talking about how everything went. "Little Audrey ate so much cake that I thought she was going to burst,"

I said, chuckling at the memory.

"She ran it all off chasing after the balloons," Joy said. "I'm glad we made the strings long enough so that the kids could reach them when the balloons floated up to the ceiling."

"It seems like each party gets better than the one before it. Remember all those disasters we had at the beginning of the summer?" Krissy asked. "I thought we were going to run ourselves out of business for a while."

"The dog jumping in Shannon Kellar's cake was the worst, but at least that seems funny now," I said. "It wasn't so funny when it happened, though."

"Just thinking about that big mutt's paws all over Abby's beautiful unicorn fantasy cake makes me laugh. Whenever I think things are going badly at school or at dance practice, I think about that stupid dog, and things don't seem so bad," Joy said.

"That's for sure!" Linda Jean commented as she walked into the room. She had been busy in the next room gathering her pets together. "You know, I think the parties are getting better because we've had lots of practice. I used to worry whether I was going to remember to tell the kids everything about my animals. Now it comes naturally. And if I forget, it really doesn't matter. It doesn't seem to be such a big deal anymore."

"Does that mean you're ready to make another chocolate applesauce nut cake?" I asked, reminding Linda Jean of her biggest fiasco.

"No way!" She laughed. "I know when I'm licked." Linda Jean had baked a chocolate applesauce nut cake for her little stepbrother, but she had left out the applesauce because he didn't like it. The result was a half-baked mess.

Abby pulled into the driveway just as we were saying good-bye to the Evans family.

"Was it a good party?" she asked.

"It was the best," I said. "I'm ready to take a nap, though."

"You can't take a nap," Abby told me. "You don't want to miss out on our traditional ice cream feast at Juliet's Family Creamery, do you?"

Juliet's is our favorite hangout after parties. It's a Party Time rule that we don't eat while we're working, and entertaining 10 or 12 kids can make you really hungry. So, at least once a week, we go to Juliet's to gorge on hot fudge sundaes and banana splits. They let you create your own dessert, so you can pile the yummy toppings as high as you want.

Fifteen minutes later, we all were enjoying our crazy ice cream creations.

"While we're here, we might as well talk about that goop goop slop party we're planning for the triplets next weekend. It's going to take us all week to get the supplies together for that one," Krissy said.

Krissy is the practical one of the group. She's very organized. She has a menu written up a week in advance for her sack lunches for school. And she has a separate notebook and schedule for each of her seven classes. Of course, Krissy is really smart. She even skipped third grade.

"What kind of physical obstacles should we have?" Linda Jean perked up. "How about knocking over baby bottles with frisbees? Or, we could toss water over their heads into a cup held in their partner's teeth behind them?"

"That sounds hard and messy," Abby commented. "Are you sure the triplets want a goop goop slop party? Do their parents know how messy a party like that can get?"

"Their mom told us the party would be held in their big backyard," Joy told Abby.

"I think we should write up a page of instructions to send to the parents. Or, we should at least send them a letter of warning," Krissy said and grinned.

I stood up, holding an imaginary scroll in front of me. I read the invisible words like a town crier. "Hear ye. Hear ye. Have your children bring another set of clothes to the goop goop slop party. Everyone WILL get messy! And be prepared to give the child a bath afterward."

Joy joined me standing up. "Warning. This party could be hazardous to your hairstyle. Please wear a shower cap and goggles."

Juliet, the owner of the ice cream shop, grinned at us from behind the counter. She thought we were silly.

Joy and I sat down. For the next half hour we came up with the most outrageous suggestions for the boys' birthday party. We were sure that they would never forget turning eight years old.

My mind began to wander as Krissy, Joy, Linda Jean, and Abby continued talking about the obstacles we would put together for the party. Somewhere between the slicked-down horizontal ladder and the baby swimming pool filled with ping pong balls, I started worrying about my busy schedule.

I tried to think of all the things I had to do next week. There was school and homework, an English test, and a report on Australia due for geography. Seventh grade was a lot different from sixth. The teachers expected much more work in much less time.

Then there was my work at the studio for an hour after school three days a week. I didn't really have specific duties the way Graham did, but I knew they appreciated me filling in where I was needed.

During the next week, I would be helping Dad gather the information for the special show on illiteracy. I thought it was neat that Dad and I would be working together on a project. Dad told me that a lot of people don't know how to read—including many kids who are graduating from high school. Dad was hoping to use his show to tell the public about the problem and what could be done about it.

I also knew I would have to attend our daily Forever Friends Club meetings at Joy's house. I had been going to Joy's house every day for as long as I could remember. Abby used to baby-sit Krissy and me when we were little. Now, she just provided a place for us to go until our parents came home from work.

Speaking of work, I was sure Abby would need our help in fixing food for all the events she was catering. Her business had grown even more than ours had.

I was thinking so hard about my crazy schedule that I barely spoke to anyone as we left Juliet's and got in the car. My head was spinning by the time Abby parked in front of her house on Honeybee Court. Krissy and I got out and walked around the circle to our own houses. We lived next door to each other at the very middle of the court.

"You must be thinking really hard," she told me. "You haven't said a word since we left Juliet's."

"I have a lot on my mind," I explained. "I guess when I get home I'm going to have to make a list. I can't keep all the things I have to do straight in my mind. Maybe if I write everything down, the list won't seem so endless."

"That's what I do," Krissy said.

"Are you having any trouble juggling all of our jobs this year? Eighth grade has to be harder than seventh," I said.

"It is harder," Krissy replied, twisting her long blond hair around her finger and holding it off her neck. "But I've learned to take things one step at a time. I set priorities for what things need to be done when."

"You mean you figure out which things are the most important, and you do them first?" I asked her.

"Yeah, that's exactly what I do. Like, I have this essay due in English. I have to read a play by William Shakespeare and then compare the behavior of the teenagers in the play to the way teenagers act today."

"When is that due?" I asked.

"It's due on Friday. But that's my point. The essay isn't due until Friday, so I'm just beginning to think about it now. First I have to study for a science test that I have on Tuesday. I really can't worry about the essay until after my science test. To help me keep track of everything, I actually put my homework schedule on a calendar."

"Wow, you write all of that down on a calendar?" I asked. "You're more organized than I am. I'm afraid that if I write everything down, it's going to seem worse because I'm going to know for sure that I don't have enough time to do everything."

"I'll help you plan it out if you want," Krissy offered.

I smiled at my friend. "Thanks. I'd appreciate that."

My family was already seated at the dinner table when I walked into the house. I took my usual seat in the middle on the left side. The smell of rare roast beef, mashed potatoes, and gravy made my mouth water. Even after eating all that ice cream, I still was hungry.

"You're just in time, honey," Mom said. She passed me the platter with the roast beef deliciously displayed on it. "Here's your favorite," she said.

"Thanks, Mom," I said.

For the next few minutes, I concentrated on piling food on my plate and enjoying my supper.

"How did your parties go today?" Dad asked. "We hardly get to see you anymore. I'm glad you're helping me out at the station, so at least I get to talk to you once in a while." He grinned to let me know he was teasing.

Randy interrupted. "Don't you know, Dad? Self-employed business owners work twice as hard as regular employees. We learned that in school today." Randy is my big brother. He's 16 years old, and I think he's pretty cool—even though he's my brother.

"That's probably true," Dad answered. "I know that I work longer hours than the camera crew does. They work a set number of hours, and my hours vary according to the story I'm working on."

My family always talks like this during supper. One of us will bring up a subject or an event, and the rest of the family jumps in to debate it. Even my younger brothers—Phillip, Doug, and Cary—get into the act. But tonight I was just too tired and worried to listen.

"What's self-employed?" Phillip was asking. He's five years old and is Doug's twin. Cary is only three.

"Self-employed means that a person has his or her own business. Aimee's business is giving parties for kids," Randy explained.

"I want a party!" Phillip yelled.

"Well, I'll see what I can do when you have another birthday. Okay?" I asked, ruffling his hair.

"Yippee!" he yelled.

"Oh, boy," said Doug.

Mom passed me the butter for the roll I'd taken out of the bread basket. "Are you sure you're not taking on too much, Aimee? Now that school has started again, you may have to cut back on the number of parties you give."

"I wish everyone would stop telling me to cut back. I can handle it. And I don't want to quit anything that I'm doing."

"As long as you can keep up with your school work, it's okay. School is your most important activity right now, you know," said Mom.

"I know, Mom. And I have a paper to write after dinner."

Suddenly, Doug started shouting. "You said we'd play Mr. Bear tonight. You said we would!" he yelled.

Phillip joined in the outburst. "Yeah. We need you to play," he said. "There aren't enough cubs without you."

Cary yelled right along with his brothers. He didn't seem to know what he was screaming about, though, because just as quickly he started to giggle.

There was so much noise at the table that I covered my ears. I didn't feel like eating, anyway. I had promised that I would play Mr. Bear with my little brothers. I looked at the clock. Playing with them would take up at least an hour, and I still had to do my report for school. I also had promised Graham that I would type up the set notes for the taping tomorrow. Graham had said that he couldn't make out the director's handwriting. Lucky for me, it was Randy's turn to do the dishes.

I knew it was useless to try to get out of playing with my brothers. They would be upset with me and make so much noise that I wouldn't get much homework done, anyway.

"Okay, you three. Who is going to be the sleeping bear first?" They chose me to be the bear first. We cleared the dishes from the table, and then I ran into the living room to hibernate. I pretended to sleep while the boys sneaked up behind me.

"Are you sleeping, Mr. Bear?" they asked in a whisper.

I snored.

"Are you sleeping, Mr. Bear?" they whispered together.

"Growl. Snarl. I'm going to get you!" I teased.

Shrieking, they scrambled in every direction, heading for home base, which was the couch. I caught Cary, but the other two escaped. Cary and I went back to Mr. Bear's den to sleep.

Over and over, we slept and chased and slept again until all the intruders were turned into cubs. Then we chose another bear. After a while, I let my worries about school and my job turn into giggles as I rolled around on the floor with my brothers. Soon, we were singing songs and clapping to the rhythm of a new marching song that I had made up.

I heard the phone ring.

"Aimee, it's for you," Randy called.

I climbed out from under the pile of cuddlers.

I reached for the phone that Randy held out to me. "Hello," I said into the receiver.

"Hi, Aimee. It's Joy. I have a favor to ask you. You can say no if it's too much trouble."

"Okay. What is it?" I asked.

"On the day of the triplets' goop goop slop party, I also have to perform in a ballet recital. My teacher just called to tell me about it."

I switched the telephone to the other ear and asked my brothers to quiet down for a minute. "I didn't think you were going to be in this recital."

"I wasn't. But I learned a few parts just in case. One of the girls sprained her ankle, and the doctor says she can't wear toe shoes for at least three weeks. And I've been picked to substitute for her."

"So, what do you want me to do?"

"Could you fill in for me on Saturday? I was going to do the train dance, but it won't work for the type of party they're having. Could you come up with something else and do my part? I'll make it up to you. I promise."

I sighed. *Just add it to the list,* I thought. I smiled into the phone. "Don't worry about it, Joy. I can handle it."

"Thanks, Aimee. You're a real friend."

"Sure. I'll see you tomorrow at school," I said.

I hung up the phone and told my brothers that it was time for me to do my homework. Then I quickly escaped to my room. I plopped down on my bed and stared up at the ceiling. *How was I ever going to find the time to do everything?*

# Three

ON Saturday morning when I woke up, I definitely could tell that fall had begun. I got up and peeked out my bedroom window. A fine mist of fog hugged the ground. I looked up into the old maple tree beside the house and realized that the leaves were already beginning to turn colors. Fall was my favorite time of year. I wondered how I had missed the first signs.

The day loomed before me. It seemed I had one busy minute after another. I quickly pulled on a pair of jeans and my Forever Friends sweatshirt. We had them made up the summer after fourth grade when Linda Jean joined our club. *Could it really have been two years ago?* I thought. I was glad we had bought the sweatshirts extra large so that we could wear them for a long time.

As I walked downstairs and into the kitchen, I saw that Dad was already dressed for work and ready to go.

"I can give you a ride to the studio if you hurry," he offered.

"Thanks, Dad. I'll just grab a granola bar and some fruit," I said. "Do you mind if we strap my bike onto the bike rack on the van? I need to leave the studio early today for the triplets' birthday."

"Of course, I don't mind. I'll do that while you're getting ready."

I ran around the house to gather up all the craft supplies I would need for the party. I was going to have the kids create their own storage containers for the ooobluck that Linda Jean was making. Ooobluck is gloppy, green, and slimy stuff that is made by adding together cornstarch, water, and food coloring. It is stringy and stretchy and gross, but it feels almost dry to the touch and is not as messy as it sounds.

I ran back to my room for an extra bottle of glue and a short-sleeved blouse in case it was a lot warmer in the afternoon. The mornings might feel like fall, but the afternoons could still be scorchers.

Dad stuck his head in the front door. "Are you ready?"

"I'm coming. Just a minute," I called. I grabbed the last of my supplies and ran past my brothers, who were just stumbling toward the TV to watch Saturday morning cartoons. Mom had already gone to work at the hospital. She's a nurse.

With my arms piled high with supplies, I climbed into the van. Dad smiled at me, waited until I had secured all my supplies, and then started the engine.

The day had begun.

I tried to use Krissy's method of setting priorities that day. As soon as we arrived at the studio, I sat down at an empty desk and made a list of all the things I had to do in the next four hours.

*Work at the studio:*

*Clean back room where props and extra scenery are stored.*

*Wash windows in Dad's office—he can't see out.*

*Help Graham with cue cards and script distribution.*

*School:*
*Finish report for English that I didn't do last night.*

*Party:*
*Plan dance to fill in for Joy.*
*Make a sample ooobluck container to show kids.*
*Leave for party at one o'clock.*

*Wow,* I thought. *How was I ever going to get it all done in practically no time?*

Graham arrived just as I was finishing my list.

"Hi, Aimee. I like your shirt. Boy, you sure are early today."

"Dad gave me a ride," I explained. Graham was wearing a nice outfit, too, but I felt funny saying that to him.

"We have a busy day ahead of us," he said. He shuffled through some papers, but didn't really study them.

"I have my list right here," I said helpfully. "What else do you have to do besides these things?"

Graham looked at my list. "Whew! That's a

lot of jobs. Well, I have to gather the props for tonight's show. We're going to need some extra tables to set all the cages on from the Humane Society."

"Oh, yeah. That's right. Tonight Dad is going to interview the director of the Society for the Prevention of Cruelty to Animals. I'm sure Linda Jean will want to watch this show."

Graham nodded. "And I have to get into that prop room and clean it up."

I looked at him strangely. "Well, that's here on the list," I reminded him.

"Oh, yeah, I forgot," he mumbled quickly.

I didn't see how he could forget that fast. He had just looked at the list a second ago. I shrugged my shoulders. I couldn't criticize him. After all, I was pretty forgetful lately, too.

"Is there anything else I need to do?" I asked.

"Mainly just pass out scripts and set up the cue cards," he said. "I guess we'd better get started."

"Would you like a copy of my list? I can make an extra for you," I offered.

"Uh, no, thanks. I'll remember—clean prop room, organize scripts and cue cards. What were the other things again?" Graham asked.

"Don't worry about the other things on the list. It's just stuff for me to do," I told him. "Okay. Let's hit it!"

That conversation with Graham turned out to be the calmest part of my morning. I washed Dad's windows first. I knew if I were him, there was no way I would be able to sit in an office I couldn't see out of.

Then Graham and I cleared out the prop room in record time. We stepped back for a second to admire our work before we dashed off again. Graham left to work on setting up the cue cards while I decided to tackle a little bit of homework.

But just two paragraphs into my report, my thoughts were interrupted.

"Could you please help me with these cue cards? Leroy has me running around doing other things, and I can't get to the cards fast enough," Graham said.

"No problem," I volunteered, setting my books aside with a sigh. Graham took off and left me with the show's script and the cue cards.

As I read the script and put the cards in order, I watched the crew. They were so efficient. Even if it looked like chaos from an outsider's point of view, I knew they each had their jobs down perfectly. Each person knew where to be at the right time so that everything flowed smoothly.

So, why was it so urgent that the cue cards be set up? They didn't usually run through the talking part of the show until right before filming. And where was Graham, anyway? This was the second time I had been stuck doing his job.

"It's great that you're getting those cue cards done so early," Ms. Moore said. "I'm so glad that you and my son are working here. You two fill a big need, and we all appreciate that."

Graham's mother seemed so emotional. Or, maybe she was just very generous with praise. She had a nice way of making everyone around her feel happy. That's probably why she was such a popular TV producer.

Graham came up to me as I was placing the last card on the rack.

"Graham," I began. "Why was there such a big hurry to get these cue cards ready? Even your mom was surprised I had them done so early."

He flapped his mouth open and shut a

couple of times, but didn't say anything. "Hang on," he said finally, raising his hand. "I really do have a reason. It's...that we have to jump on our bikes and spend the afternoon buying all the things that your father needs for tonight's show. He gave me a list," he said, handing a list to me.

"Animal stickers for the studio audience, tape, fish food, flea soap," I read. "We'll have to ride all over town to get this stuff."

"That's why I need you," he pleaded. "If I have to do this alone, it will take all day. But together, we can get it done in only an hour or so."

"Then we'd better get going," I said, heading for the door. "I have to be at a party at 1:30."

"I'm sure we'll be back by then," Graham said.

I took one last look at my unfinished homework that was stacked neatly on Dad's desk. "Boy, I hope so," I said. I knew what the Forever Friends would think if I was late again.

I looked at my watch. The digital numbers said 11:45.

"We should split up," I told him. "I'll take half of the list. You take the other half. It's the only way we'll get everything done."

"No," he said loudly. "Uh, we can do it together. One of us can watch the bikes while the other person goes into the store. It will save time by not having to lock and unlock our bikes. Besides, I don't know where all these places are."

"Didn't they give you a map?" I asked curiously. *Why was he so panicky about shopping alone?*

"Well, sure, they did," he said, waving it at me. "But it's more fun to shop with a friend."

His smile was contagious. "All right, Mr. Helpless. I'll do it. But we have to be back by 1:00."

Off we went on our bikes, whizzing through several neighborhoods and skirting around Calvary Park. We stopped first at the pet store, and then we went on to the stationery store. The list seemed endless, and all I could see in my mind were the angry faces of Linda Jean, Joy, and Krissy.

Finally, we finished the errands. With our backpacks bulging with supplies, we raced on our bikes to the fountain in Grant Square.

"Wow. I never thought we'd get it all done," Graham said with relief. "I couldn't have done it without you, Aimee."

"That's because you made me do all of the work. Here's your list back," I joked. "Next time, I'll stand with the bikes, and you can go into the stores and do all the buying."

"We had fun, though, didn't we?" Graham asked sweetly. "This is the best job I've ever had. It's much better than raking leaves or walking people's dogs. Which do you like better, WBCC or Party Time?"

"Oh, no!" I exclaimed, looking at my watch with horror. It was already approaching 2:00. Where had the time gone?

"I'm half an hour late! The party has already started!" I yelled.

"I'll ride with you and explain it to them. They can blame it on me," he offered.

"No, you have to go back to the studio. Here, take my pack. I'll just ride straight to the triplets' house. My friends are going to be really angry!"

I had never ridden four miles so fast in all my life. The wind whizzed through my hair. Still, it was almost 3:00 when I arrived, panting at the Cranston's front door.

As I turned the knob on the door, I realized that I had left all my craft supplies at the studio. My Forever Friends were going to be really upset with me.

Linda Jean and Krissy had the boys and their friends under control when I walked in. Or, they were as much under control as 12 kids could be when they're tossing playing cards over their heads into a basket.

Cards flew through the air and were followed by shouts of "Hurray" and "He did it."

"You'll never make it, Jamie!" Ronald shouted. "You'll never beat my record of 10 cards."

Linda Jean looked up at me from where she sat on the kitchen stool. "Well, look who finally decided to show up," she sneered. "Are you sure you can find time in your busy day for the rest of us?"

"I'm really sorry," I told them. "Hi, kids!" I yelled to the noisy group of boys.

"Well, at least you're in time to do the craft part," said Krissy from behind her clown's face. "We've played all the other games. All that's left is crafts, dance, and food. We even had the boys open their presents already."

"We opened presents before we got all dirty," Tommy added with a big grin.

"That was smart," I joked, hoping to lighten

the mood and wipe the frowns off Krissy's and Linda Jean's faces.

All the kids were wet and slimy from head to toe. I guess they were mostly wet, because the green ooobluck was the only slime. And it seemed to be sitting in small globs all over the kitchen table.

"Well, are you ready to do the crafts?" Krissy asked. She looked down at my hands and saw that I didn't have my backpack with me.

"As a matter of fact, no," I said softly. "I was in such a hurry to get here that I left my backpack at the studio."

"That's okay," Andy, one of the triplets, said. "We have baggies."

*What a sweet little boy,* I thought. *He's trying to make me feel better at his birthday party!* But Linda Jean and Krissy clearly were not going to get over it that easily.

"It's time for the dance," Linda Jean announced.

I slapped my head with my hand. "Oh, my gosh. I knew there was something else I forgot!"

"You have to be kidding," Linda Jean whispered. "You're late, and then you forget all your stuff and the dance, too? Why did you even bother to come?"

Linda Jean turned to Krissy. "What are we going to do with the last half hour of the party?" she asked.

"What about...?" I started to say as I walked up behind them.

They kept their backs turned.

"Forget it," Krissy said. "You've done enough damage already. We'll figure out something. Why don't you go back to Graham and the studio?"

"Because I'm a part of this business, and I'm here to help," I replied sternly.

"You could have fooled me," Krissy said.

"It seems to us that you're going to have to make a choice," Linda Jean continued. "You'll have to choose either the Forever Friends Club or Graham and the studio. You don't have time for both."

"I think she's already made her choice," Krissy said, staring right at me. Then she turned to the kids who had just finished bagging up their ooobluck.

"Where's the record player, Joey? Do you have any marching music?" Krissy asked him.

Joey showed her where the record player was, and then he ran off to get the music.

Meanwhile, Krissy explained her impromptu dance to the group.

"I'm going to turn the music on. Everybody dances while the music is on. Then, when I turn the music off, you have to freeze like a statue. Got it?" she asked the group.

"Yeah!" they all shouted.

I stood by the leftover refreshments. I was alone. No one paid any attention to me or asked for my help. I wasn't needed there.

I felt really awful. And I was the only one to blame.

# Four

I spent the rest of the party trying to make amends. I jumped wholeheartedly into the statue dance. The kids laughed, but Krissy and Linda Jean just looked the other way. I even did my best to do more than my share of the clean up. But nothing I did worked.

It was obvious that Krissy and Linda Jean weren't speaking to me. I figured that Joy would know soon, too. And then she would ignore me, too.

*What was I going to do?* I was so confused. It just didn't seem fair that I'd have to choose between my Forever Friends and Graham and the TV studio. But the real problem was that I didn't even have time to find solutions.

I still had to ride back to the studio to get my books so I could get my homework done before the evening was over. And we had two more parties scheduled for Sunday. *How fun would the parties be if the Forever Friends were all angry with me?*

I thought about not going to the parties at all. But I had to go. After all, I was part of the team whether the other three liked it or not. I would apologize and promise never to be late again. And hopefully they would forgive me. That was what I would do.

Still, I couldn't stop thinking about my problem. I rode my bike back to the studio more slowly than usual and blocked out most of my surroundings in my mind.

As soon as I got home and sat down to do some homework, Mom called me for supper. The meal of spaghetti with parmesan cheese and garlic bread looked good. But my stomach rumbled in protest each time I tried to swallow. *Hey, maybe I'm getting sick,* I thought. If I got sick, I would have had a real excuse for not going to the next two parties.

I excused myself from the table and walked to my room. I tried hard to throw myself into finishing my English report. Finally, after an hour, I had a final draft. I closed my book and slumped across the bed.

My eyes closed, and suddenly I couldn't hold the tears back any longer. Tears gave way to sobs. After a while, I lay still with my face in the pillow.

I heard a light tap on my door. "Are you asleep?" Randy asked in a whisper.

"No. I'm just resting my eyes," I told him. We had repeated this same exchange since we were kids. It didn't matter if either of us was studying or sound asleep. It was something that we shared.

"Flooding your eyes looks more likely," he said, bending over to peer into my face. "Why have you been crying?"

I started to say, "Oh, it's nothing," but one look into his worried eyes, and I knew it was all right to tell him the truth.

"Linda Jean and Krissy are really upset with me," I told him. "Joy probably is too by now."

"All friends have little fights sometimes," Randy said. "This will probably all blow over by morning."

"I doubt it. This wasn't just a little fight."

He sat down beside me on the bed. "Do you want to tell me about it?"

I know not all big brothers are like Randy.

I guess I was pretty lucky that he cared enough to ask.

"I've been working at the studio, you know, to help Dad."

He nodded.

"Today I got stuck downtown helping Graham gather props for the animal shelter show Dad did tonight. I got so involved in running errands that I was late for the party, and I forgot my stuff. I even told Joy I'd cover for her dance this time, and I got so busy that I forgot."

"But being late for one party doesn't seem like a good enough reason to stop speaking to you. What are they going to do, give all the rest of their parties in silence?"

I giggled. He made it sound pretty funny, even though it wasn't.

"The trouble is that this wasn't the first time I'd been late. At the studio I've been doing my work and helping Graham with his, too. And I'd shown up late to so many club meetings that they changed the meeting time. But it seems that I'm still letting them down."

"Why?" Randy asked.

"They said that ever since I met Graham, I've been neglecting them. They told me I had

48

to make a choice between Graham and the Forever Friends Club. How can I make a choice like that? They are all my friends," I explained. I felt like I was going to cry again.

Randy thought for a minute. "New friends really complicate things," he said. "When I started hanging around Marcy Williams, some of my buddies got angry. But, they got over it later after they found girlfriends of their own."

"But Graham isn't my boyfriend," I protested. "He's just a friend. I like spending time with him. We have fun. We like to do the same things. But the girls think I'm ignoring them."

"You are, sort of," he told me, leaning back against the wall. "You used to spend all your time with Krissy, Linda Jean, and Joy. Now you want to take some of that time to spend with Graham. Do you think they could be jealous?"

"I don't think so," I said after thinking about it. "I think they're just angry because I'm not holding up my end of the business. I know if I learn to manage my time better, these messes won't happen." I snapped my fingers. "Maybe that's the way to show the girls that I'm really serious." I pulled a piece of paper out of my binder. "I'm going to call Krissy right now and ask her to help me organize my schedule. She already told me she would help if I needed her."

"That's great," Randy said, getting up from the bed. "But I still think you should have a talk with them. Maybe you all have started to expect too much from each other. You guys are growing up. Other things are bound to take time away from the group—especially boys. You shouldn't have to choose between Graham and your other friends," he concluded as he left me alone to call Krissy.

When Krissy answered the phone, she acted cool at first. But she did agree to help me become organized. As soon as I hung up the phone, I ran to thank Randy. Then I walked through the backyard and jumped over the fence into Krissy's yard. I walked in Krissy's back door to her kitchen.

Kitty, Krissy's little sister, was sitting at the kitchen table.

"Hi, Aimee! How's show biz?"

"I should be asking you," I told her. "I saw the commercial you did for Crispy Toasty Wheats last night. You looked great."

"Thanks," she smiled her million-dollar model's smile. "I just wish someone would call me for a real part. I'm getting tired of being the little kid on cereal commercials."

I laughed. "You are a little kid," I said. "You can't expect to be a movie star when you're only nine years old."

"I know. I'm practicing for my fabulous career in the future." She grinned. "If only they'd cast me in a sit-com, then I could play the role of a bratty little sister or something."

Yes, you could. In fact, you could play that part very easily," Krissy teased as she walked in. "You'd make a perfect little brat." Then she ruffled Kitty's hair to show Kitty she wasn't serious.

"Speaking of fabulous careers," I said, "I'm going to have no career if I don't learn how to manage my time better. I have a thousand things to do, and no time to do them. Please help!"

"Do what I do. Get an agent," Kitty offered.

"Yeah, I wish I could have an agent," I said.

"It's almost that simple, Aimee," Krissy said. "But you don't need an agent. You just need an appointment book. I brought mine out for you to look at. And I have an extra one for you to take with you."

She handed me a small notebook. The cover

had the picture of roses in bloom. Inside, the pages were divided into squares, one for each day of the week. When the book was opened flat, you could see the whole month before you.

I read what she had written in the first few squares. "Monday—band practice. Take extra reeds for clarinet. FFC meeting 5:00 p.m. Tuesday—pick up highlighting pens when supply shopping. Begin research on history assignment (library is open until 9:00 p.m.). Wednesday—dentist appointment. Come home early from club meeting to start dinner."

"See. It's easy if it's all written down. Then you don't have to try to keep everything in your head at once," Krissy explained. "You can relax and do only one thing at a time."

"Wow! You're as busy as I am," I said.

"No, I'm not. But I was last year when I was trying to be in honors club, computer club, band, the youth symphony, Forever Friends, and do homework. But I decided I was doing too much for the wrong reasons," she said, looking at Kitty. "Finally, I dropped about half of my activities. Life is a lot easier for me now."

Krissy had spent all last year thinking that her parents liked Kitty better because she is a famous model. Krissy almost went crazy trying to prove herself until she and Kitty straightened things out.

Kitty tapped me on the hand. "I have to turn down lots of jobs because they cut into my schoolwork," she told me. "People just can't do everything, and do it well."

"I can't believe I'm taking advice from a fourth grader," I said.

Kitty folded her arms across her chest. She looked hurt.

"But it's good advice," I said quickly. "I just don't know what activity to drop from my schedule. I want to do everything."

I started to make up a list of all the things I do each week. I included all of the school assignments that I knew were coming due and all the parties that were scheduled.

Kitty was bored by the time she got to the end of the second page. She wandered off into the living room. That was when I decided to level with Krissy.

"I just can't make a choice between the Forever Friends and Graham," I started.

I hesitated, watching Krissy's face closely. She kept it blank, waiting for what else I had to say.

"You didn't really mean it when you said I had to choose, did you?" I asked.

Krissy let out her breath in one big puff. "I think...we really meant that you have to be committed to the club above all else. It especially applies if we're going to run Party Time. We have to be able to count on you."

"I know. And I promise to do my best. I will make sure that Party Time is always my number one commitment," I said. "Do you think it would help to call Linda Jean and Joy and talk to them, too?"

"Talking isn't going to do much good," Krissy said flatly. She picked up my list and began entering the items that I had written in the extra notebook. "Follow through on your end of the business, and that will be proof that you mean what you say. Show up on time, and do your job. That will show all of us that you are serious about it."

I nodded, and I knew that she was right. But as I penciled in all of my activities and deadlines, I began running out of space in the squares. I sure hoped this organizational stuff would work. But glancing at the month, I didn't see how it could. I didn't have a single day or moment free.

# Five

THE parties on Sunday went pretty well. But Linda Jean was still kind of angry with me for being late to the party the day before. And Joy couldn't believe that I'd forgotten to make up a dance. At least Krissy had cooled down a little.

The kids all loved the games and crafts and dances, so that was the high point of my day.

On Monday, I turned in my report. It felt good to have it done on time. Then I remembered that I had told Mom I would baby-sit Doug after school. I dashed home to get Doug before I had to leave for the studio.

"Come on. Get your shoes on. We're going to be late," I told Doug.

"I want to stay home and watch cartoons," he declared.

"You can't stay home. No one is going to be here to watch you. I promised Mom that I'd take you to the studio with me this afternoon," I tried to reason with him.

"I don't want to go," he whined.

I smiled, fighting to stay calm. "It'll be a lot of fun hanging around a TV studio. Don't you want to see all the cameras and help Graham with the sound effects machine? You can even watch Dad work."

Doug tilted his head to the side and looked like he was considering his choices. He didn't realize that he only had one choice.

"Okay, I'll go." He paused. "But I want to take some goodies and my building toys with me."

"It's a deal," I said, slipping on and tying his shoe before he had a chance to change his mind again.

Actually, he really didn't have a choice. Mom had taken Phillip and Cary to the dentist. Randy had to stay after school to paint signs for the dance that was coming up, and Dad was at work. And I had to go to the studio. So, I'd told Mom that I'd take Doug with me.

Doug packed his suitcase of building toys and stuffed a paper bag full of pretzels and fruit into the corner compartment. He closed the lid and flipped the latches closed.

"I'm all ready," he said.

"You look just like a business executive," I said. "It looks like you're carrying your brief-case to a big office downtown."

"I am going to work," he informed me. "I have to build a space station with my toys for Ryan when he comes over Saturday."

I smiled. *If only my life could be as simple as my five-year-old brother's is*, I thought. I pictured the schedule that Krissy had helped me write out, and I knew that if I stuck to it, I would be able to make my life simpler, too.

We were still teasing each other as we walked into the studio and met Graham at the door to the prop room.

Doug saluted Graham. "Major Doug reporting for duty, sir!"

"You've been watching too much television," I told him.

Doug just grinned.

"Where does he get this stuff?" Graham asked me.

"He gets it from Randy, I think. Or, maybe he learns it from the kids at kindergarten. Who knows? Ever since he started school, he seems to be growing up so fast."

Graham cleared off a low table for Doug to put his building toys on. Doug set out his plan book with all the different toys shapes. Next to it he set his gray base boards that would be the bottom of his space station, and a paper cup that he filled with water.

"What's the water for?" Graham asked. "Is it supposed to be a pond?"

"No. It's in case I get thirsty," Doug explained reasonably.

I laughed and looked at Graham. "You fell right into that one, you know."

"Hey," Graham said. "I know a trick with a glass of water and two spoons. Do you want to see it?" he asked Doug.

"Sure!" yelled Doug.

I stood back and watched Graham entertain my little brother. *That's another reason I like Graham*, I thought. *He's kind, and he likes to make people laugh.* I always feel special when Graham is around.

"This is what you do," Graham was saying. He had two teaspoons balanced on each other and a glass of water sitting a few inches away.

"You slap the top spoon like this, and the other spoon flies into the water glass." He banged his fist on the top spoon. The bottom spoon went sailing into the air, past the water in the glass, and landed on the floor.

"You missed," Doug and I said at the same time.

Graham held up his hands for silence. "No problem. I just got distracted. I'll make it this time."

He set the spoons up again and banged his fist down. The bottom spoon just lay there. The top spoon flipped over, and he caught it in his teeth.

Doug giggled. "You missed again."

"But this time it was on purpose," I said.

"No, it was an accident," Graham pretended. "Just give me one more chance. May I have a drum roll, please."

I tapped out a rhythm on the table top with my fingers.

This time the trick worked. The spoon flew up in a perfect arc and splashed into the water glass.

"Wow!" Doug exclaimed.

"Hey, that was great!" I added.

"Do you want me to do it again?" Graham asked.

"Yeah!" Doug yelled.

"Forget it, Graham. We have to work," I said, shaking my head. "But we sure could use you at our parties. The kids would love that trick."

"I can tie a cherry stem into a knot with my tongue, too," he informed me.

"Oh, that would be thrilling. I'm sure they'd be impressed," I said, teasing him.

We worked quickly through the rest of day. Graham seemed to take for granted that I would organize the cue cards while he passed out scripts and props. He had managed to weasel out of that job, but I didn't mind. I liked reading the cue cards to find out what each show was going to be about.

The show we were preparing for was about illiteracy. The show would stress how important it is to be able to read.

As I scanned the script, my mouth fell open. I couldn't believe how many people can't read. The script said that 25 million Americans can't read at all, and another 35 million adults can only read at the fourth grade level or lower. People even have died because they couldn't read the labels on cans in the supermarket. They buy poison instead of food.

"This is really awful," I told Graham when he joined me. "Can you believe all the people in the United States who can't read?" I showed him the figures. "I thought everyone could read. I mean, I knew that some kids had trouble, like those who live far away from schools or who are very poor and have to work instead of finishing school. But the script says that illiteracy is almost at epidemic proportions."

"Yeah, right. Well, listen, is everything under control here? I have a load of homework to do tonight," Graham said quickly.

"*You* have homework?" I exclaimed. "I've never seen you even open a book."

He did a little spin, finishing with a bow. "That's because I'm such a whiz."

"What do you have to do?" I asked.

Graham showed me his books. "This is my math book. I'm taking pre-algebra."

I looked at the math problems he had to do. They were much more advanced than ones I had to do.

"I've never tried any pre-algebra problems before," I said.

"Here. Let me show you," he offered.

Once Graham had explained the variables and the equations, pre-algebra seemed easier than I thought it would be.

Everything was going fine until we hit the word problems.

Graham studied the problem for a long time. Finally, he said, "Okay, smarty, try this one."

"What does it say?" I asked, waiting for his response.

He shoved the book in front of me. "You read it," he said.

I shoved the book back toward him. "You read it. It's your homework," I teased.

Again, the book came back to me. "If you don't read it yourself, you won't understand it. That's the way word problems are."

"Fine," I said. "If you insist."

I read the problem out loud. "An express train travels 150 miles in the same time that a freight train travels 100 miles. The express is traveling 20 miles per hour faster than the freight. Find the rate of speed for each train."

"That's easy," he said. Graham began to write the numbers down on his paper.

"I'll race you," I challenged. I grabbed an extra sheet of paper and wrote out the equation. Graham finished before me. He was twirling his pencil in his teeth when I finally looked up.

"The freight train's rate is 40 miles per hour, and the express train's rate is 60 miles per hour," Graham stated proudly.

"That was harder than I thought it would be" I admitted. "I only got as far as writing the equation."

"That was an easy one. Read the next one." He leaned forward, waiting for me to read the problem to him.

"Forget it," I told him. "Do it yourself. I have enough homework of my own. I have to be getting to the Forever Friends Club meeting, anyway."

I started gathering together my books and my brother's backpack and latest building creation. Graham came up behind me and brought the book around in front of my face.

Come on, Aimee, old pal. Read just one more word problem," he begged. "We were having fun."

"I know. But I do have to leave. I promised Krissy I'd be there on time today. Hey, Doug, are you ready to go?"

Graham got down on his knees. He held his hands up to me with his math book in them.

"Please, Aimee. I just can't do my homework without you!" he said dramatically.

I couldn't tell whether he was joking or not. He had a silly grin on his face, but the tone of his voice was serious.

I laughed it off. "If I didn't know better, Graham Moore, I'd think you didn't know how to read. Maybe you should be on the literacy special."

Graham was on his feet in an instant.

"Fine!" he said. "Don't help a friend. Who needs you, anyway?"

He grabbed his books and stomped off into the soundproof listening room before I could say anything else.

"Is Graham upset?" Doug asked, returning from the conversation he had been having with some of the stagehands on one of the sets.

"I don't think so," I told him. "He's probably just fooling around."

I looked back over my shoulder several times to see if Graham would stop pretending and wave good-bye to me.

But he didn't.

# Six

AS Doug and I left the TV studio and headed for Joy's house, I couldn't stop thinking about Graham. He had reacted so strangely to my teasing about the literacy program. *Was Graham just fooling around, or was he really upset? And what was there for him to be upset about?*

Joy's little nephew, Jeremiah, was supposed to be visiting, so I knew that my brother would have fun entertaining the baby at Joy's house.

"Can you believe it?" Linda Jean asked. "The long lost Aimee Lawrence has arrived on time."

"I've already told you that I'm really sorry," I said. "Krissy has helped me write down my schedule. So, I hope I can keep everything

65

better organized now."

I showed them my new schedule, which I had taped to the inside cover of my binder. "I have another copy on the front of the refrigerator at home and a third copy on my bedroom door," I said.

"Boy, you are busy," Joy admitted, looking at my schedule.

"Well, I plan to live up to my end of the business," I said. "And I don't plan to mess up again like last Saturday. I really did just lose track of time."

"Just let us know ahead of time if you can't make it to a party, or if you are going to be late," Krissy said.

"I will," I said.

We spent the rest of the afternoon planning our two weekend parties and a slumber party the next Friday night. By the time the meeting had ended, we all seemed to have put our fight behind us. I just hoped I would be able to keep up with everything.

By Friday, I was sure my new schedule was working great. I had managed to get my homework done on time, attend all of the Forever Friends Club meetings, volunteer at the studio, and cheer up Graham.

On Friday, we taped the final interview for the literacy special. Dad, Graham, and I watched the completed show in the viewing room with the crew.

"Sixty million Americans are functionally illiterate. They either can't read at all, or they read below the level necessary to function successfully in our society," Dad said in his opening remark.

He continued, "Here with me today is Margaret Phillips, a reading consultant and literacy specialist with the federal government. She pioneered literacy programs in several states, including the most successful one in California called Project Read. She is currently awaiting state funding to begin a Project Read program in Georgia. With the help of trained volunteers, Ms. Phillips hopes to duplicate the success of the California program in teaching people to read. Ms. Phillips, tell us how the Project Read idea started."

Ms. Phillips talked about the first Project Read class that was held in the community room of a small California library. Her story was fascinating. She alone taught 20 people to read. After that, she got the idea of asking for help from the government. The government then hired her to go from state to state to create more programs.

"People who cannot read come from all walks of life," she said. "They are not stupid. Many hold good jobs or get good grades in school. They all have one thing in common, though. Each has his or her own methods for avoiding reading or for getting along without reading."

"But why is it that people don't learn to read?" Dad asked Ms. Phillips. "Has the school system failed them?"

"Reasons for not reading are as individual as each person. Perhaps a child was ill during a critical stage in the learning process. Perhaps a physical problem went undiagnosed, such as poor eyesight or impaired hearing. Perhaps a person is dyslexic, which means he or she sees letters mixed up in different ways than you or I do. Frequent family moves, overcrowded classrooms, dropping out of school, and drug usage are all causes for illiteracy."

Graham crossed his legs and wiggled his foot up and down. He twirled a string around his fingers.

"It looks good. What do you think?" I asked Graham.

He looked up at the screen. "Yeah. It's a great show."

"You're not even listening to it," I accused.

"I'm sorry," he grinned. "I have other stuff on my mind."

"Like what?" I asked him in a whisper.

"Like how to get this rubber band off my fingers without using my other hand." He held up his hand. A rubber band was hooked around his little finger and stretched across the back of his hand to his thumb.

I laughed softly. "Use your teeth," I suggested, and then I went back to watching the tape of the show.

Ms. Phillips was using a chart to explain some statistics about illiteracy. The red line on the chart showed that illiteracy was on the rise. She said, "About 2.3 million people join the pool of functional illiterates each year. It's not a pretty picture, especially since many people who don't learn to read also can't get jobs and end up living on welfare. Do you know that over half of the people in prison can't read? I think that is an alarming statistic."

"What should a person do if he or she

suspects that a friend or co-worker can't read?" Dad asked her.

Ms. Phillips took a sip of water and continued. "First let me tell you about some of the signs to watch for. People who can't read tend to ask people to do their work for them. It's especially true when that work involves reading. They don't like to shop because it usually involves reading labels. Cooking may be difficult if there's a recipe to follow. They have to have a navigator along on a car ride because they can't read the street signs."

As she read down her list, I looked over at Graham. He was using a piece of tape to pick the lint off his navy blue cords.

Ms. Phillips continued, "Also, beware of the fellow student who always requests help with his homework or who makes silly mistakes and covers for them with a joke," Ms. Phillips explained. "We discovered that one boy couldn't read when he kept going into the wrong bathroom in the school."

Suddenly, things started to fall into place in my mind. I thought back over the events of the last few weeks, and I began to get suspicious of Graham's behavior.

Graham had gone into the wrong store the

other day when we were buying props. The list clearly said hardware store, but he had gone into the bicycle shop. I had thought he was clowning around again and checking out the new bikes. Well, that was what he had said, anyway.

And hadn't he slyly gotten me to do his cue card job? What about the list of jobs I wrote out the other day? He read the list, and then he added jobs that were already written down.

Graham got up to get a drink of water. He seemed a bit nervous.

*Did this show make him nervous?* I wondered.

Then, suddenly, I remembered the night Graham was upset because I wouldn't help him with any more algebra problems. Maybe he hadn't been kidding when he begged me to help him. He had whizzed through all of the math until he got to the word problems.

I studied him as he bent over for a second drink. *Could it be possible that Graham didn't know how to read?* I thought.

"Since Project Read isn't officially set up in Georgia yet," Dad's TV voice broke into my thoughts, "where can people go for help?"

"There are several options," Ms. Phillips

said. "The easiest thing to do is to contact a counselor at your nearest school. Adults should contact counselors at the high school or college level. Children should talk to a teacher or counselor they trust at their own school."

I couldn't stop thinking about Graham during the rest of the show. Everything that Ms. Phillips said seemed to fit. I thought that even the way Graham was trying to avoid listening to the show could mean that he was embarrassed to admit his problem.

After the show, I looked straight into Graham's eyes, hoping he would say something. But he just laughed and said, "I'll see you Monday."

I rode my bike home, ate dinner with my family, then walked over to Joy's house. Abby was going to give us a ride to the Bradleys' for the overnight birthday party that Party Time was giving for Theresa Bradley. The Monday before, we had planned all kinds of fun things for the slumber party. I just didn't know if I had the energy to give a party.

"Is something bothering you?" Joy asked when I walked in.

"It's nothing that a few giggling, screaming, crazy nine-year-old girls won't cure," I replied, trying to put on a cheerful face for the party.

The slumber party would be the best thing to take my mind off my troubles. Well, they weren't troubles exactly. They were just concerns about Graham.

The Party Time crew arrived around 7:00 at the Bradleys'. Kids began arriving a half an hour later.

"This is pretty late for nine year olds to have a party, don't you think?" Linda Jean asked.

"Theresa's mother said that Theresa always stays up late on Friday and Saturday nights," Krissy said.

"I was never allowed to stay up all night when I was nine," I told them.

"Let's hope it's not all night," Joy said. "I was hoping we could get them to sleep by 11:00 or 12:00."

"Good luck," Mrs. Bradley remarked, joining us in the entryway. "The last time we had an overnight party, the girls were up until 3:00."

Silently, I hoped that wouldn't happen this time. I wanted to get up early the next day to try to learn more about illiteracy. I wanted to find out something that could help Graham.

The more I thought about it that night, the more I was convinced that Graham couldn't read. I kept remembering little things, like scripts that Graham had given to the wrong people and props that he had put on the wrong shelves. And he never did his homework in front of me, except that one time. I liked Graham too much to stand by and not do anything to help him.

*Aimee, concentrate on the party,* I told myself. *You'll have tomorrow to worry about Graham.*

Krissy already was performing her routine. Her clown outfit was decorated in slumber party fashion. Curlers stuck out from her orange wig. She had small cotton rolls between her toes as if she was getting ready to polish her toenails. And she wore a brightly colored bathrobe over her checkered pants.

"Hey, gang," Krissy announced. "I am now going to do the amazing linking rings trick. Never before have you seen pink linking rings, I'll bet."

The kids all shook their heads.

"Here's what I'm going to do. You examine

this one," she said, holding the first ring out to Theresa, the birthday girl.

"You check out this one," she said, handing the second ring to Margaret.

Krissy pretended to link two rings together and hand them to someone else for inspection. I went into the dining room to get ready for the craft activity.

We were going to make pajama bags out of cloth. The kids were going to draw on the bags with fabric crayons. Then we would iron the design to melt it into the fabric. Mrs. Bradley had said we could use her sewing machine to stitch up the sides and the drawstring top.

Luckily, Theresa had only invited five girls to her slumber party. This kind of project only worked with a small group.

I spent the next hour helping the girls complete their pictures and sew up their bags.

"Wow, that's terrific, Shelly. You're very creative," I told the tiny dark-haired girl. She was smaller than the other nine year olds, and she was very artistic. The detail she had included on her pajama bag was amazing.

As I ironed her design, I could tell the colors would stand out vividly against the white background.

"Oh, it's beautiful!" Shelly exclaimed. "It's too pretty to put my pajamas in it. I'm going to use it for a purse."

"That's a great idea," I told Shelly.

You can use your bags for anything," I said to the group. "Pajamas were only a suggestion. This is a good way to make decorative pillows, too. One year I gave all my friends pillows made just the way we're making these bags."

I really enjoyed working with Theresa and her friends. It was great to take our time and not be rushed through a party like we were with younger kids.

"Are you guys ready for a facial?" Linda Jean asked the group.

"Go ahead," I told the girls. "I'll clean up here."

"Thanks," Theresa said.

They ran off to join Linda Jean in front of the big bathroom mirror. For an overnight party, Linda Jean had decided it would be too much of a hassle to bring her animals. Besides, girls would be more interested in makeup and facials, she decided.

Since her mom moved to Atlanta, Linda Jean had learned a lot about putting on facials and makeup. This was her first chance to use the activity for Party Time.

A few minutes later, the girls all came back to the living room, wearing egg-white masks on their faces.

"Lie on the floor until the mask dries," Linda Jean instructed. "And whatever you do, don't laugh."

Of course, that started everyone giggling.

"You look like a ghost who swallowed an ice cream cone," Theresa told Margaret.

"You should see yourself," she retorted. "I think a giant jellyfish attacked your face."

"Okay, women," Linda Jean said. "The mask won't work if you talk or laugh. You'll crack it."

They were silent after that. Only an occasional giggle escaped.

"What is that mess you smeared all over them?" Joy asked. "Does it really work?"

Linda Jean stuck out her chin. "Of course, it works. Nine year olds don't have any wrinkles, but it will make their skin really clean and soft. It's made of all natural stuff, like beaten egg whites, powdered milk, and honey."

"Who taught you how to do that?" I asked.

"My mom showed me," she explained.

"Are you glad your mom moved back to town now?" Krissy asked.

Linda Jean smiled. "Yeah, I am. I know how upset I was at first, but I think things have turned out great. It's really nice having Mom around to ask about girl stuff. Dad's the best, but he certainly isn't helpful about girl stuff! And you know how much I love Josh and Stephanie. Steph was so cute when she called me on the phone the other day."

Listening to Linda Jean talk about her stepbrother and stepsister made me think about Doug. Ever since we had spent the afternoon at the studio, Doug hadn't stopped talking about Graham. He wanted to know when they could play together again.

A few days ago, I probably would have felt free to invite Graham over to my house. But now I wasn't sure that I could face Graham without asking him if he could read. I knew that I had to do something soon. But what?

# *Seven*

AFTER school on Monday, I called Dad at the TV studio to tell him that I wouldn't be in to work because I had an important errand to run. All day at school, I had avoided Graham so I wouldn't have to lie about why I was skipping work.

Dad didn't seem to mind, so I felt a little relieved. I gathered my books from my locker and headed to the guidance counselor's office.

I had never been to the guidance counselor's office before. It was really neat. Posters hung on every wall. There were lots of books and even a tray of cookies.

"Mmm," I sniffed. "Cookies and books are my favorite combination!"

"Hello." The woman behind the desk smiled

and stood up to greet me.

"Hi. I'd like, uh, I came to ask you a few questions."

She smiled. "Sure. Just have a seat. That's what I'm here for."

She passed me the plate of cookies and waited for me to continue.

"I'd like to speak with someone about learning to read," I said.

"You've come to the right place. I'm Mrs. Lansky."

"I'm Aimee Lawrence," I said. "How do you go about teaching a person to read?" I blurted out. "I mean, are there special books or lessons? Does someone have to read kindergarten books to learn to read?"

"No," she explained. "I give each person who comes to me a thorough screening to determine the cause of his or her reading problem. Then that student is paired with a tutor."

"What if the person is too embarrassed to come to you? Do you have any tips for studying at home?" I asked her.

"I suggest that you make an appointment. Your reading problems may be more complex than can be handled at home," Mrs. Lanksky told me with a smile.

Suddenly, I realized that she thought it was me who couldn't read.

"I didn't come for me," I told her. "I have this friend who has a reading problem. At least, I think he does. I heard Ms. Phillips, the reading consultant from Project Read, talk on *Weekend Mag* the other night. And my friend does the things she said means a person can't read."

"What kinds of things are you talking about?" Mrs. Lansky sat back in her chair to listen.

"He's been asking me to help him with homework that involves reading. And he went into the wrong store the other day. He was really fidgety when we were watching the show about illiteracy. I think he was scared someone might find out that he can't read."

"It sounds like your friend needs to talk to me himself," Mrs. Lansky said, leaning forward in her chair. "Having a reading problem is nothing to be ashamed of. But knowing you have a reading problem and not taking the steps to correct it can be much worse. I won't make your friend feel self-conscious. I promise."

"What if he won't come?" I asked her. "Isn't

there some way for him to study at home? Couldn't I help him?"

"The best help you can give your friend is support. Support him in the decision to get help," Mrs. Lansky said. She handed me a packet of literature about learning to read and a sample workbook that she uses to help people learn to read.

"How can I find out for sure? I mean, should I just ask him if he can read or not? Should I try to trick him into admitting it?" I asked.

"Sometimes confronting the issue head on is the best way. But he may not be honest if you just ask. He probably has been hiding his problem for a long time. And his pride is involved," she said thoughtfully. "Maybe you can put him in a situation where he would have to read something. Perhaps then he would admit his problem."

She pointed to the top paragraph on the brochure. "For example, you could say, 'I have something in my eye. Could you read this for me?'"

Mrs. Lansky looked at me and waited. I realized she was still testing me about whether I could read or not.

"I really *am* here to help a friend," I told

her. "I can read fine. In fact, I love to read." I decided to demonstrate my ability by reading the first paragraph so she would take my problem with Graham seriously.

She laughed. "Okay, I believe you." She smiled. "You have to realize that a lot of people ask me for information for a friend. And then the friend turns out to be that person."

I nodded.

"Just remember that you can't teach your friend to read by yourself. Even if you did use the workbooks and methods that I use, learning to read can take a year or longer. The process takes a lot of time and energy and commitment from a tutor."

I picked up the literature and stood up. "I'll find out first if my suspicions are true. Then I'll convince him to come to see you."

"Good luck," she called after me.

I made it to Joy's house in time for the Forever Friends Club meeting. I hid the information brochure in my backpack. I wished I could talk to all of them about my suspicions about Graham, but I knew that Graham would be hurt if he found out I had told my friends about his problem.

*Keeping secrets isn't easy*, I thought.

At the meeting, we all talked about how tired we were at Angela's party on Sunday after having been at Theresa's slumber party on Saturday night.

"I think we did pretty well at Angela's party yesterday, considering we only got five hours of sleep the night before," Joy remarked.

"I don't know," Krissy admitted. "I was so tired that I'm not sure what costume I had on."

"I don't know how you girls do it," Abby said, coming into the room. "Do you think you have enough energy to help me make a few batches of pizza pinwheels for the Garden Club meeting tomorrow night?"

"Of course," we all said, taking our usual places around the kitchen. We put on our Abby's Catering aprons and stuffed our hair up into our hair nets. Then we took turns washing our hands.

"Don't the members of the Garden Club ever get tired of eating pizza pinwheels? We make them for almost every meeting," Linda Jean said.

Abby handed her a bowl and wooden spoon.

"Nope. Ever since you made the mistake of spreading pizza sauce instead of brown sugar on the cinnamon roll dough, pizza pinwheels have been the Garden Club's favorite. They request them every time."

"It's a good thing you made that mistake," Joy said to Linda Jean.

"Do you think you girls could help me serve at the meeting? Feel free to say no if you have too much homework," Abby said.

"You know we can always fit Abby's Catering into our schedules," Krissy assured her. "It's no problem."

"Tomorrow night is fine for me," said Joy.

"It would be fun," Linda Jean replied. "What about the kids? Will they be at the meeting this time?"

"Not this time," Abby said. "I just need you to serve, not entertain."

I was busy mixing dough and wondering how I would fit the meeting into my schedule. Krissy seemed to have read my mind because she walked up beside me. She sprinkled cheese on the dough I'd just prepared with pizza sauce and whispered, "I'll look at your schedule and figure out a way to fit the Garden Club in."

"Thanks. I don't know when I'm going to study for my math test," I confided.

"Maybe I can quiz you while we work. I'll give you problems, and you can solve them in your head. It will be good practice," she suggested.

"I still have to stop at the studio after school tomorrow. I have something very important to do that can't wait." That statement sounded more mysterious than I had wanted it to.

Krissy looked at me with one eyebrow raised.

"I can't tell you what I'm thinking about," I said. "Not yet, anyway."

I had a plan. Well, it was sort of a plan. I just knew that I had to find out for sure whether Graham could read.

I arrived at the studio before Graham did the next day. My plan was to look really busy when he entered the studio. I waved to Dad and to Graham's mom.

Dad motioned me over to him.

"Before you get caught up in cue cards or whatever," he said, "I'd like you to do a favor for me."

"Sure, Dad. What is it?" I asked.

"The show this week is about the new French bakery on Peachtree Street that is getting rave reviews. I'd like you to call them and ask for a menu to be sent right over. Also, if you have time, I'd like you to call up three other bakeries and ask for their prices of the items on this list," he said, handing me a piece of paper. "We're going to do a little comparison shopping."

"How about a little comparison tasting?" I asked, licking my lips.

"I'll keep you in mind if that job should come up," Dad said with a grin.

"Hey," Ms. Moore interrupted. "I thought taste testing was going to be my job."

When I walked away, they were still arguing about who liked French pastries more.

*This will work out perfectly*, I thought. I'll be busy making phone calls, and Graham will have no choice but to arrange the scripts with the cue cards.

"How's it going?" Graham greeted me.

I put my hand up to show him I was talking to someone on the phone.

The cue cards sat in a neat pile next to me. The script was on the top of the pile.

Graham ignored them. He waited for me to get off the phone.

"Thank you very much," I said to the clerk at the French bakery. "I'll meet the delivery person at the door."

"What are you up to?" Graham asked as I hung up the phone. "Is it anything I can help with?"

I shuffled a few papers, looking as busy as I possibly could.

"Gosh, Graham. Dad asked me to make a bunch of phone calls for him today. He says they are urgent. You'll have to do the cards and scripts today. I'm sorry."

He looked at the scripts. Then he looked back at me.

"Uh, well, what about the props?" Graham stammered.

"As far as I know, the bakery is bringing the only prop, a big basket of bread," I explained as calmly as I could. I dialed as I spoke. "Listen, I really have to get back to these phone calls if I'm going to finish them all today. Shhh, it's ringing."

I shrugged my shoulders, talked on the phone, and waited for Graham to make a move. He picked up the script, scanned it without really looking at it, and put it down again. He turned to walk out the door.

Then, without even planning it, I had the perfect test for Graham.

"Yes, just a minute," I said to the woman on the phone. I covered the mouthpiece and called to Graham, "What does that top line on the piece of paper say, Graham? Dad wanted me to price all the items he listed there. But I can't remember the first one."

He started walking toward me, holding the piece of paper in his hand.

"Just read it to me," I said. "I've remembered the rest, and this woman is waiting."

Graham looked at the paper. His mouth moved, but no words came out.

"Come on, Graham. She's waiting for me."

The paper shook in his hands. He tried a few times to make the word come out. Then he shook his head.

"You think you're so smart!" he yelled. "That's a great trick! You finally got me."

I didn't say anything.

He threw the papers across the room. Cardboard and typing paper scattered everywhere.

"I can't read! Are you happy now?" Graham practically screamed.

"I'll get back to you in a little bit," I told the woman who had been holding on the phone. Then I hung up.

Graham slumped in the chair by the door.

I walked over to him, wondering what I was going to say. I realized that I had been hoping I was wrong about Graham. Trying to find out his secret was one thing, but now that the truth had come out, I was scared.

"I'm sorry, Graham. I suspected you couldn't read, but I didn't know for sure. I admit I was trying to find out," I said softly.

He rested his forehead in his hands. "Why?" he wailed. "Now everyone is going to find out. My mother will find out. I might as well crawl into a hole."

Graham was usually so happy and full of fun. I wished I could take away the hurt.

"I won't tell anyone," I promised. "But you should tell someone. I can't believe your mom doesn't know. How did you manage to get by all this time without her knowing?"

He looked up at me. Two tears trickled down his cheeks.

I put my hand on his shoulder.

"My mom doesn't know because I've always lived with my Dad, except during the summers. Dad figured my grades were low because I changed schools so often," Graham explained. "We always moved before a teacher had a chance to tell him. Besides, I do get decent grades in some subjects."

"Yeah, but you get those grades by having other people do your work for you," I accused. "You're not dumb, Graham. I've seen you whiz through your math problems. And you juggle everyone's props and manage to get them to the set on time. You have to be pretty smart to do all that without reading."

"I do have a good memory," he said, smiling slightly.

"Then why can't you read?" I asked. "Reading is mostly memorization and sounding out words."

He put his head in his hands again. "I don't know. I wasn't there when they taught a lot of stuff. I missed school a bunch when I was little. One time I had hepatitis, and another time I had pneumonia. I almost died once."

"Well, you could have caught up with a little extra help," I began.

"You don't understand, Aimee. My dad didn't have time to teach me to read. He was hardly ever there. When he was on assignment, I had a nanny who stayed with me. Boy, did I hate her. She made me eat peas."

That image seemed so ridiculous that we

both burst out laughing.

"Please don't tell anyone about this," he said, straight-faced a moment later. "I'd die if anyone knew."

"Why don't you go to the guidance counselor's office at school? She can help you. She'll even get you a tutor."

"Are you kidding? Then my mom would find out for sure," Graham said. He looked terrified.

"What's so bad about that? Your mom would understand and help you." I searched his face, trying to understand why he was so afraid of being found out.

"Mom would be ashamed of me. Just look at her," he said. "She's perfect. She has a fancy job and knows all kinds of important people. What's she going to do with a son who can't read? She'll be so angry."

I shook my head. Graham was wrong, but no matter what I said, he wouldn't listen to me.

"Please, Aimee. You're a good reader. You could help me. You could study with me. I'd learn. I promise. Then no one would have to know." He was begging me.

"Well, I suppose I could use some of my

brother's books and give you a few tips," I offered.

"Oh, thank you, thank you," he said, hugging me. "You won't regret this. I'll bring my homework to the studio. I'll come over to your house after work. I'll come over on weekends."

"Whoa! Wait a minute, Graham. I have a lot of other things to do, too. I can't spend all my time tutoring you. In fact, I'm not sure I really have any time to spare."

Just as quickly as he had become happy, Graham slumped back down into the chair. He looked defeated. His voice was so soft that I almost didn't hear him ask, "Please?"

Then he looked up at me. His hand reached out to touch mine. I couldn't just ignore the pleading expression in his eyes.

Could I?

# *Eight*

IT seemed like confronting Graham had become a mission for me. And now that I knew
for sure that he couldn't read, my life had become even more complicated.

Keeping a secret from my Forever Friends
was really hard for me. We were used to sharing
all our joys and problems. They were used to
me bursting into the room and telling them
all about my day.

But now I just went to our meetings. And
I did my part for our parties. But I didn't know
what to say when we talked. I was afraid I
would tell them about Graham.

By the time the week was up, Krissy, Joy,
and Linda Jean were upset with me again.
They said I wasn't paying attention to my job
because I hurried through my crafts projects.

Krissy was the only one who knew how crazy I was feeling. But even she didn't know that every day I sneaked some early reader books into my backpack. The last 10 minutes before my hour was up at the studio, Graham and I used the books to help him learn to read.

He was doing great on the children's books, but he still couldn't read the directions for his homework or write a simple essay. I did all that for him, too. Between doing my own homework and Graham's eighth-grade homework, I was completely worn out.

On Friday afternoon, I almost fell asleep in class.

"Are you all right?" Krissy asked when I saw her later on the school steps.

"Uh, yeah, I'm fine," I said, trying my best to act energetic. "Actually, I'm a little tired. I think I better go home and relax for a little while. I think Randy will be home to watch the boys so maybe I can get some sleep."

"What about the bike ride we all had planned for this afternoon?" Krissy asked.

"You'll have to count me out. I'm not up for anything today, the meeting or the studio. I think I may have the flu."

I slowly stumbled home. Exhausted, I

barely said another word to Krissy.

"Take care of yourself," Krissy said as she left me at my door. "Remember the space program party at Eric's house tomorrow. Abby's catering the party, so remember that we're getting together early to help her make the food. It's on your schedule. Call me later to let me know how you're feeling."

"Okay, Krissy. Thanks. I'll make it to the party. I'm sure I just need some rest."

"I'll tell Joy and Linda Jean that you won't be coming on the bike ride," she said as she walked down the sidewalk.

The others would probably think I was avoiding them like I had all week. I couldn't help it. I knew if I really let my guard down, I would tell them about Graham.

"What I need is an afternoon off," I said to myself as I hung my windbreaker on the rack in the hall when I got home. Four pairs of sneakers were lined up against the wall. I added mine to the row.

"Hi, everybody," I said, entering the kitchen for a snack. "If you need me, I'll be in my room. But try not to want me," I told them.

*I'm not being very responsible today,* I thought. I pulled my school clothes off and slipped into my sweatpants and my Forever Friends sweatshirt.

On my bed, I laid back and stared at the ceiling. Graham and Dad will wonder where I am. The Forever Friends will be angry that I didn't go riding with them. And I know what my English teacher would think if she knew that I stuffed my book under the bed.

I pulled my basket of yarn off the hook on the wall. Ever since I hung my craft supplies from the ceiling, Mom hadn't said a word about my messy room. But I had been so busy that I hadn't even worked on a project since June.

My life definitely had gotten out of hand. It seemed that so much of my time was promised to other people that I had no time for myself anymore.

I flipped through a pattern magazine and chose a small needlepoint design that was a key chain with the picture of a rose on it. I cut the plastic canvas to the proper size and began stitching.

My needle flew faster and faster. Red yarn quickly filled in to form a rose.

Suddenly, I missed a stitch and stabbed my finger.

"Ouch!" I yelled to myself. Tears swam in my eyes.

There was a knock on the door. I quickly rubbed my eyes and sat up straight as Mom opened the door and walked in.

"I came to see if you were feeling okay," she said. "Randy said you were acting a little strange earlier."

I forced a smile. "Everything is fine, Mom. I just needed some privacy."

"What beautiful work you do," she said, picking up the rose I was making. "You really like needlework, don't you?" Mom asked.

"Yeah. Doing it gives me a chance to think," I told her.

"You must be thinking pretty hard. You've almost finished the design. Is there anything you want to talk about?"

She rubbed the back of my neck. As the tension eased, I realized how easy it would be to talk to Mom about my problems, about being overloaded, and about Graham's reading problem. I wished that I hadn't promised to keep everything a secret.

"I don't really feel like talking," I lied. "Everything is fine. I'm having a great time at school. The studio is interesting and fun. Of course, the parties are keeping me pretty busy."

"It sounds to me like you're overworking yourself," Mom said with an understanding smile. "Are you sure you're not doing too much? Maybe you should drop some of your activities to give yourself a rest."

I shook my head. "No, Mom. I don't want to drop anything. I'm fine, really." I jumped up and did a tiny jog around the room."

I thought I was very convincing.

"In that case, can I ask you a favor?" Mom asked. "I'd like to go have my hair done. And Randy needs a break from watching the boys. Do you think you could watch your little brothers until Dad gets home. He said he would bring dinner home tonight."

"Sure, Mom," I told her. "I'll be out as soon as I put away my stuff."

Mom left and closed the door behind her. I put my face into my pillow and sobbed.

"What am I going to do?" I cried. "I'm falling apart, and there's no one to catch me."

"Come on, Aimee. Come play red light, green light with us," Phillip said from the doorway. Behind him stood Doug and Cary.

I stopped crying. "The sun has gone down,

and it's getting cold out," I said, stalling while I wiped my eyes.

"We can play in the hallway. You can be the light post," he said.

"Okay." I went to the end of the hall and stood with my back to them. I wiped off the last of my tears. I didn't want to let my little brothers down.

"Green light," I said. "Red light!" I turned around and caught Cary trying to sneak up on me. "Go back to the beginning," I ordered softly.

I turned back around. "Green lizards. Caught you, Doug. Go back. I didn't say green light. Ooops, I guess I did."

They started running.

"Red lighthouse," I said.

They stopped, but they started again when they realized I hadn't said the right words.

"Red light!" I shouted.

We continued to play, but my heart wasn't in it. Finally, after 10 minutes, I decided to make a snack and sit in the living room by the TV. The boys joined me for a little while.

Finally, Phillip said, "This is boring. Let's play hide and seek."

"Or, we could play bunny, bunny, where's

your tail!" yelled Doug excitedly.

"Let's do cut and paste," demanded Cary.

"Go do whatever you want," I said. "I'm resting."

"You're not supposed to rest. You're supposed to play with us," Phillip explained seriously.

"You be the baby-sitter for a while. I'm tired."

"You can't be tired—" Doug started to say.

"I said to leave me alone! Do you hear me?" I practically yelled at them.

I instantly felt horrible. I hardly ever yell at my brothers.

"Hey, I'm sorry, you guys. I guess I do want to play hide and seek, after all. Then we'll cut and paste or do whatever you want, okay?"

"Hurray!" they yelled, running back to my side. They jumped all over me, hugging and tickling me.

I spent the rest of the afternoon trying to make up for shouting at my brothers. I don't think they noticed how tired I was. As soon as Dad came home from work, I went straight to bed. I didn't even bother to eat dinner.

# *Nine*

B Y Monday, I felt a little calmer than I had on Friday, but I was still exhausted.

"Another week of school ahead of us," I said and let out a big sigh. I put down my lunch tray on the cafeteria table and piled my books beside me on the floor.

"Didn't you get caught up over the weekend?" Krissy asked. "You look like you're doing homework for two people."

*If she only knew,* I thought. I didn't answer her comment. More and more lately, it seemed that I had to ignore what people said to me. I knew Graham's secret would come tumbling out if I talked much at all.

Instead, I focused my attention on some commotion across the room.

"Isn't that Graham?" Joy asked.

"He's probably doing his cherry stem trick," I said, trying not to look interested.

Graham stood up on the bench as the crowd gathered around him. They all cheered him on as he wiggled the tiny stem in his mouth to tie the knot.

"How does he do that?" Linda Jean wondered. "Have you asked him?"

"I don't have time to ask Graham about his stupid tricks!" I snapped. "I have enough problems of my own."

"You don't have to bite my head off, you know," Linda Jean snapped back.

"I'm sorry. I'm just on edge."

"You're always on edge these days, Aimee," Joy told me.

"I'm not doing it on purpose. I'm trying my best," I said, raising my voice. "Let's just eat, okay? I have to eat and go do some homework before my next class."

I didn't tell them that I had to get my own homework done now so I could do Graham's later. I bent my head over my notebook and scribbled down the answers to the review questions for my history class.

Joy flipped her hair back and turned away from me. "Okay, don't talk to your friends.

Who are *we* compared to Graham the Great and your fancy job at the TV studio?"

"Look, I'm following Krissy's schedule. I've made it to all the meetings on time lately. I've made it to all the parties and held up my end of Party Time. I'm not trying to ignore you. I'm just trying to get all my work done," I said to all of them.

"That's fine," Linda Jean said again. "That's just fine. Don't let us bother you."

It seemed like every time I opened my mouth, someone got angry. So, I decided to be quiet.

I looked over at Graham again. *Why did he have all the fun?* I asked myself. *I struggled to do all my work, plus help him with all of his. He should be spending his lunch hours studying,* I thought sourly. Instead, he had a good time while all my friends got angry because I was ignoring them.

Graham's lunch room act was the last straw. After he finished his tricks for the day, he walked casually over to our table.

"Hi, Party Timers. Did you see my new trick? It's the one where I take a rubber band off my ear without using my hands," Graham said.

Suddenly, I was furious. "How long did it take you to learn that trick, Graham?" I asked him as calmly as I could.

He grinned his special warm-your-heart grin at me.

I wasn't moved. "How long did it take you, Graham?" I demanded.

"Aimee, what's the matter with you?" Krissy whispered, alarmed by the tone of my voice.

"Nothing's the matter," I said. "I just want to know how many hours Graham had to practice the rubber band trick to get it right."

"It took me six hours to learn it," he replied. "The guy who taught it to me said it took him a week."

"Shouldn't you be using some of those precious hours to do your homework? I mean, I have a lot of homework," I said, pointing to my open books. "And you're in eighth grade. Your classes must be much more difficult than mine are."

"What's your point?" he countered, matching my gruff tone. In his eyes I saw a mixture of anger and fear. He was afraid I was going to blow his cover. He knew I had power over him, power to ruin his image at school. But

I wasn't mean, just very angry with him for using me.

"Oh, there's no point," I said sweetly, smiling at his puzzled expression. "I was just curious. Well, I'm done for the day. How about a walk?" I directed my suggestion to only the girls.

"That's a good idea," Krissy said. "We'd like to talk to you."

"I'd like to talk to you, too," I said, staring directly at Graham. "There are some things I'd like to clear up."

"Aimee," he called after me.

"I'll see you at the studio, Graham," I said.

"I'm sorry for the way I acted in there," I said as soon as we were outside of the cafeteria. "There's something I have to tell you all."

Linda Jean was walking next to me. She stopped. "What is it? You were pretty hard on Graham in the lunchroom. We get upset with him because he seems to take up a lot of your time, but you were more than upset."

By then I had calmed down enough to know that I shouldn't just blurt out the news that Graham couldn't read.

"You're right. Graham has been taking up a lot of my time, and it's going to stop. But I can't tell you yet everything that has been happening. There's not enough time, and," I looked around at the crowds of teenagers, "school isn't private enough."

The bell rang to signal that lunch period was over.

"You can't leave us hanging. Give us some kind of a hint," Krissy said.

"I promise I'll tell you about it at the meeting this afternoon. It's only fair to Graham that I warn him first," I said.

I knew I sounded overly mysterious, but I couldn't help it. I had to talk to Graham first, so he would know that telling his secret wasn't just out of anger. I wanted him to know how concerned I was about him. I wasn't a tattle-tale. But his secret had become too much for me to handle alone.

The hardest thing I ever did was face Graham that afternoon. He came into the studio as silent as a mouse. He did his job on one side of the prop room, and I did my job on the other.

Ten minutes before quitting time, he sat down next to me with his homework.

"Are you still angry? Will you help me read my homework?" Graham asked softly.

I squeezed my hands tightly in my lap. "No, I'm not angry. And no, I will not read your homework for you."

"It sounds like you're still upset with me," he said, standing up and looking away.

I walked around in front of him. "Graham, don't you see? You're not learning anything when I do your homework. I've been feeling like a crazy person trying to keep up with all of this, and you're just sailing along without a care."

"That's not true. I care about you, Aimee," Graham said defensively.

"Don't change the subject. Your problem is a lack of responsibility. I know you can learn to read. I've seen you progress quickly when you feel like it. But most of the time you're too busy learning stupid tricks and entertaining your friends at school to learn how to read." The more I talked, the more angry I became.

"Can't a guy have any fun?" Graham asked.

"You're using me, Graham," I said. "Do you think *I'm* having fun? All of my friends are angry with me for neglecting them. I don't have any time for my brothers. I'm a mess, and you're doing tricks on benches in the cafeteria. Does that seem fair to you?"

Graham shook his head. "You offered to help me learn to read. And now you're backing out."

I sat down. This was harder than I thought it would be.

"Listen, Graham. I'm not giving up on you. I'm getting smart. Mrs. Lansky, our school counselor, told me I couldn't teach you to read by myself. She was right. It takes a long time and a lot of patience."

"So, you think I'm a hopeless case?"

"No. I think you need a tutor, not a sympathetic friend," I said. "I just can't do it anymore."

I got up to leave.

"What am I supposed to do now? There is no one else I trust." He reached out and put his hand on my shoulder. "You can't leave me with all this," he said, picking up and dropping his book bag.

"Tell your mother," I said. "Talk to Mrs. Lansky. Get help. It's your life and your problem. I'm your friend, Graham. But I just can't do this anymore."

"Go ahead! Run off to your *real* friends!" Graham shouted after me.

I turned around one last time. "I'm *your*

friend, too. And so are Krissy, Joy, and Linda Jean if you would give them a chance. They won't like you any less because you're just now learning to read. I'm going to the Forever Friends Club meeting right now. I'm going to tell them what has been going on. They've been upset with me for acting so crazy all the time. I have to tell them about everything."

He stomped past me out the door. "You're a traitor, Aimee!"

"Tell your mother," I whispered after him, tears filling my eyes. "Please tell your mother. She'll understand."

# Ten

JOY opened the door before I had walked halfway up the driveway.

"What gives?" she asked as the others followed her outside onto the porch.

"Yeah, what's the big secret?" Krissy asked.

Linda Jean was silent.

"Let's talk about this inside the house," I said. I looked around to see if, by some slim chance, Graham had followed me. I didn't see anyone around.

I hoped I was doing the right thing by telling the Forever Friends about Graham.

Once we were settled inside the house, Abby brought us hot chocolate and homemade pretzels. She sat down to listen, too.

"This must be important if you had to wait until you were all alone," Abby said softly. "Do

111

you mind if I stay? I've been very worried about you."

"No, I don't mind. I'm really sorry I've kept this from all of you. It's just that Graham made me promise not to tell anybody. Now I know I should have asked you for help from the beginning."

"Ever since you were little, you always wanted to solve your problems on your own," Abby observed. "Maybe this problem is just too big."

I took a giant gulp of air. I felt like I was betraying Graham. I remembered the hard look in his eyes when he had stomped off earlier. I knew I had lost him as a friend. And that hurt a lot.

"Does Graham know you're telling us now?" Linda Jean asked.

"I told him. He wasn't very happy about it. I wanted him to come, too, but he was too upset. And he didn't think you would understand."

"Tell us about it, Aimee," urged Joy. "We'd like the chance to help you if we can."

"Well, do you remember the show on literacy that my dad did a little while ago?" I asked them. They all nodded, and I continued.

"Graham had been doing a lot of things that seemed a little odd to me, but I never questioned them. But during the program, Dad's guest, Ms. Phillips, told all the signs to watch for when someone may be covering up a reading problem."

"Graham has a reading problem?" Joy asked.

"Yeah, but it's more than that. He never really learned to read at all. I finally tricked him into admitting that he can't read. At first, he was angry, but then he asked for my help. So, lately, I've been trying to teach him to read. And I've been doing all the homework for both of us."

"I just can't believe it," Linda Jean said. "Aimee, I think that's really something that you'd help him like that."

"So, what's Graham going to do now?" asked Abby. "Will his parents help him?"

I spent the next hour telling them about my suspicions and how I had figured out the truth. I told them about talking with Mrs. Lansky at school and how she had warned me against trying to solve the problem myself.

It felt so good to be sharing everything with my Forever Friends and with Abby.

Later that evening, Graham called me. At first, I was nervous because I had no idea what he was going to say. But, to my surprise, he sounded happy.

"Aimee, I took your advice and talked with my mom," Graham said. "She couldn't believe it at first, but the more I talked, the better things seemed. She's going to help me find a good tutor. I just called to thank you for being honest, even if it did hurt a lot to hear the truth."

For the first time in a long time, I felt weightless and free. "I told the Forever Friends about everything this afternoon. Everyone understood, too. I think you should get to know Linda Jean, Joy, and Krissy. You may just like them."

"Yeah, you're right. I guess I'm getting used to the idea that a lot of people are going to find out about my secret," Graham admitted. "You know, it's kind of a relief."

\*　\*　\*　\*　\*

As fall turned into winter, I saw less of Graham. Instead of working at the studio right after school, Graham had been going to Mrs.

Lansky's office to meet with his tutor. As I'd be leaving to go to my Forever Friends Club meetings, he'd be arriving at work. We waved to each other in the halls at school. And on weekends I was busy with Party Time parties.

"You see more of Graham than I do," I complained to Krissy at one of our Forever Friends meetings.

We were planning a Christmas party for the children at the hospital.

"I can't help it if we're in some of the same classes at school," she teased.

"He calls you on the phone, too," I said a little defensively.

"He only calls to make sure of homework assignments. All he does is ask about you after he understands all the homework."

"Really?" I asked. I couldn't hold back a grin.

"You should be proud of him. His reading is really improving. He even raised his hand to read directions out loud in class the other day."

"That's great. I'm really happy for him. I just miss him." I looked over at the others. "I miss all those tricks he did in the cafeteria and how he always entertained my brothers when I brought them to the studio."

"I have an idea," Joy said. "Let's invite Graham to the Christmas party at the hospital. He can do his tricks for the kids. They'll love it. And it'll be a good chance for you to see him, too."

I jumped up, excited. "I'll call him right now. Hey, I know," I said as I dialed his number. "We can ask him to be the narrator for the Christmas play."

Graham was thrilled when I invited him to the party. I couldn't wait to see him. This was going to be the best party ever. We had been making decorations for weeks. We even had decorations to donate to the hospital. They were made by the kids during some of our parties.

On Saturday, the day of the party, we all gathered at Joy's house in our matching Forever Friends sweatshirts. We loaded up the decorations, the crafts, Krissy's Santa clown suit, Joy's elf outfit, and Mac, Linda Jean's macaw. She had taught Mac to sing "Jingle Bells" for the kids.

Graham met us at the hospital. He was dressed all in white, with a big top hat made of cardboard and covered with silky material. He carried a small white suitcase.

"Wow, you're really ready to give a show," I said.

"Only the best for my best friends," he remarked. "You look like a rainbow," he told us, looking from one sweatshirt to the next. "Is everybody ready to sing?" Krissy asked.

"Sure. One, two, three," I counted.

"Deck the halls with boughs of holly," we sang as we entered the lobby.

A few of the nurses came out from behind their desks and sang with us as we marched through the lobby to the elevators. Krissy handed out candy canes to the people we passed in the halls. And I rang the sleigh bells as background music.

The kids were ready for us on the third floor. Twenty children were gathered around a big tree in the playroom.

"Hi, everybody. Merry Christmas. Happy Chanukah. Happy birthday. Happy New Year," I said.

The kids giggled despite their wheelchairs and bandages.

"I just wanted to make sure I wished you a happy everything," I told them.

Soon, Linda Jean, Graham, and I were helping the children trim the tree. Krissy and

Joy went to change into their costumes. I took a small group at a time aside to decorate their beds and wheelchairs. I painted ornaments, snowmen, and santas on their cheeks or casts.

"Hi, Lydia," I greeted a girl who looked about six years old. "What would you like me to paint on your face?"

"I want a teddy bear," she said. "Mine has to have surgery." She held the stuffed animal out to me.

"He does?" I asked. "Do you have to have surgery, too?"

She nodded, and her shiny dark curls bounced. "We have to have our tonsils out."

"That's not so bad," I told her bear. "Lots of little bears have their tonsils out. You'll be home before you know it."

"Really? Teddy wants to go home," Lydia said.

"Do you want me to paint a tiny ornament on his nose?" I asked her.

She smiled and handed me the bear. I painted a tiny star on her bear and a matching one on Lydia's nose.

Joy clapped her hands as I finished. "I want all of you to help me," she said to the group. "I usually do a dance, and all the kids at the party join in. But this time," she said, looking around at their expectant faces, "the nurses and doctors will have to dance instead."

"Yeah!" the kids shouted.

"No, no, not us," one doctor said.

"But the dance won't work without you," Joy insisted. "Just give it a try. May we have some music, please?"

Graham flipped a switch, and the sound of tinkling bells and flutes filled the air.

"Just follow me," Joy said, and she began to spin and leap across the floor. "This is the Follow the Elf dance."

For the next few minutes, Joy wove in and around the happy children. The nurses and doctors following Joy were not very graceful, but the kids loved watching them.

"Are you ready for your act?" I asked Graham as I slipped into a chair next to him.

"I'm as ready as I'll ever be," he said. "I may be a little rusty. I haven't performed in a while. I've been too busy reading."

I raised my eyebrows and nodded. "You'll be great," I said.

As soon as the dance ended, Graham jumped to his feet. Actually, he was only on his feet a second before he stood on his head.

"I'll bet you've never seen a person drink a glass of water while standing on his head," he said to the group.

Wide-eyed, the kids all waited to see what he would do. Graham motioned for a cup of water and proceeded to spill it all over his face.

The kids giggled.

"No way. You can't do it," taunted a red-haired boy named Raymond.

"Watch me," Graham said. This time he drank the water to huge applause.

"He's great," Krissy said. "We should have him come to parties more often. He has all those kids trying to flip spoons into their water pitchers. Raymond almost has it."

I watched as Krissy cheered on Graham. "I guess you like him now," I said. "More than before?"

She continued to watch his antics as she answered. "Yes, now that I know him better, I think he's pretty nice."

I sighed. Krissy saw Graham all the time. They were both in eighth grade. They had the same classes and the same homework. She understood his problem with trying to please his mom better than the rest of us did. *Maybe Graham was more Krissy's friend than my friend now*, I thought.

"I guess I'd better go set up for the play," I said a little too quickly. Immediately, Krissy could sense that something was wrong.

Krissy put her hand on my arm. "Wait a minute. Do you think I like Graham as more than just a friend?" she asked with concerned eyes.

"It's okay. Really," I told her. "We were never more than friends."

Krissy laughed. "You're crazy. I'm not going to date him or anything. Besides, all he talks about is you. I told you that before. I'm sure you're still his number one friend." Then Krissy went off to check her makeup.

"Thanks," I said as she left. "I think."

I don't know why I was feeling so sad. I knew I had done the right thing by advising Graham to seek help from a tutor. But when I was his secret tutor, I was really special to him. He needed me more than anyone else. Part of me, the selfish part, wanted to go back to that time.

"This is no time to be in a bad mood," I mumbled to myself as I set up the props for the play. "We're here for the kids."

I took extra care to talk to each child as I

brought all their wheelchairs into a semicircle for the performance.

"Wow, you're looking very strong," I said to Raymond.

"The doctor says I'll be home in time for Christmas," he said, beaming.

"That's great." I couldn't help but smile. He was such a cute boy.

"What a pretty dolly," I told a little girl with a row of stitches healing on her forehead.

"She has a concussion, too," she said, showing me the small bandage on the doll's head that matched her own bandage.

I kissed the doll's head. "I hope she get's all better soon."

For the next 15 minutes, we entertained the kids with a funny version of Santa's Workshop. Graham read the narration, and we acted out the parts of silly elves. The kids giggled and cheered.

Later, as we finished cleaning up, Graham's mother came to pick him up.

"You have to go home already?" I asked when I saw Graham's mother walking down the hall. "I was hoping you could go to Juliet's Family Creamery with us for our after-party celebration.

"Of course, he can go," Ms. Moore said as she walked up behind me. "I didn't come to take him away. I came to thank you, Aimee."

The Forever Friends and Graham gathered around as Ms. Moore pulled a small gold box out of her purse.

"Graham and I both want to thank you for caring enough to help so much," she said. "I know how hard it must have been for you to try to teach him to read, and especially for realizing that the problem was too big for you to solve on your own."

Ms. Moore put her arm around Graham's shoulders and continued, "Graham and I are much closer now. And we have you to thank for that."

I shook my head. "Graham did most of it. I just yelled at him a few times," I said, teasing him.

"If it hadn't been for your yelling, I probably never would have learned to read," said Graham. "You can't imagine how reading has opened up the world to me."

"Boy, this is getting mushy," Linda Jean said. "Open the box, Aimee."

"Are you all in on this?" I asked, looking around at their faces.

"Just open the package," Graham said with a grin.

I tore off the ribbon and opened the box. Inside, on a bed of cotton was a tiny gold chain. The charm hanging from the center of the chain said "#1 Friend!"

"I was afraid that I had spoiled the surprise earlier when I said that you were still Graham's number one friend," Krissy said.

I looked up into Graham's shining eyes. I wanted to hug him, but I just stood there, smiling and crying at the same time.

"We have another surprise," Joy said, when I didn't say anything.

"Another surprise?" Graham asked. "Do I know about this?" he asked his mother.

Ms. Moore shrugged and shook her head.

"Graham, we have a present for you. We'd like to make you an honorary member of the Forever Friends Club." She pulled out a colorful sweatshirt that matched the ones we usually wore.

I brushed my tears away. I took the sweatshirt and held it up in front of Graham. Then I really did hug him, shirt and all.

"I can't think of anything I'd like better," I said.

Graham smiled. The tips of his ears turned red. "Wow," he said, pulling his new sweat-shirt over his head. "Neither can I."

**Look for these other books in
The Forever Friends Club series:**

#1 *Let's Be Friends Forever!*
#2 *Friends to the Rescue!*
#4 *That's What Friends Are For!*
**coming soon:**
#5 *Friends Save the Day!*

# About the Author

CINDY SAVAGE lives in a big rambling house on a tiny farm in northern California with her husband, Greg, and her four children, Linda, Laura, Brian, and Kevin.

She published her first poem when she was six years old, and soon after got hooked on reading and writing. After college she taught bilingual Spanish/English preschool, then took a break to have her own children. Now she stays home with her kids and writes magazine articles and books for children and young adults.

In her spare time, she plays with her family, reads, does needlework, bakes bread, and tends the garden.

Traveling has always been one of her favorite hobbies. As a child she crossed the United States many times with her parents, visiting Canada and Mexico along the way. Now she takes shorter trips to the ocean and the mountains to get recharged. She gets her inspiration to write from the places she visits and the people she meets along the way.